Mistletoe & Matches

A Tangled in Tinsel Novelette

Sereyna Vale

Self-Published

Copyright © 2025 Sereyna Vale

All rights reserved

The characters and events portrayed in this book are fictitious. Any similarity to real persons, living or dead, is coincidental and not intended by the author.

No part of this book may be reproduced, or stored in a retrieval system, or transmitted in any form or by any means, electronic, mechanical, photocopying, recording, or otherwise, without express written permission of the publisher.

ISBN: 9798276326429

Cover design by: Sereyna Vale
Printed in the United States of America

For the witches who stir their tea clockwise for luck. Who believe in love spells and blanket forts. Who also know that some fires are meant to be tended, not tamed.

Contents

Title Page
Copyright
Dedication
Foreword
Winter Witchcraft   1
Sparks and Spells   5
Rules, Rivals, and Almost Kisses   8
The Long Night and the Match   21
Mistletoe and Matches   27
Epilogue: One Week Later   33
Bonus Chapter!   36
Afterword   41
Acknowledgement   43
About The Author   45
Books By This Author   47

Foreword

If you're reading this, you've officially been lured into Hollysin Town. Where the snow is thick, the cocoa's spiked, and the locals take mistletoe very seriously.

This story started as a holiday fling between a witch with a stubborn streak and a firefighter with one hell of a smirk... and then it caught fire. Add in one precious six-year-old, a cat with too much personality, and a blizzard that doesn't know when to quit, and you've got yourself a perfectly chaotic Christmas.

So buckle up buttercup. Things are about to get witchy, witty, and just a little bit wicked.

Winter Witchcraft

Ivy

The scent of cinnamon and clove fills the chilly December air as I arrange bundles of dried herbs and crystal charms on the small wooden table of my booth. The Mistletoe Mischief Festival in Hollysin Town is already buzzing. Twinkle lights were strung overhead, the scent of hot cocoa curling from every vendor cart, and laughter spilling over from the skating rink. It's my favorite time of year, chaotic and comforting all at once.

"Don't knock over the sage again," I warned softly, glancing down at the giant ball of fluff sprawled across a box of spell jars. My Maine Coon, Hexley, blinks slowly looking unimpressed, before stretching his tail directly into the display. "You're doing this on purpose," I scolded him.

I love this little booth. It's a small piece of my shop — **Wicked Brews & Charms** — and every year it draws a steady stream of curious tourists and local regulars. I offer enchanted tea blends, protective amulets, and tiny spell kits. Each item is infused with intention and love. People might not believe in magic, but I do. I like to think that Hollysin Town has a little of its own.

"Miss Ivy!"

I didn't need to look up to know who's calling. Sophia Wilder barrels toward me in a blur of puffy purple coat and missing front teeth, her grin was contagious. Six years old and unstoppable. She's got the soul of a storm and the heart of an empath. She's been sneaking over to my booth since the festival opened.

"Hey, Little Witchling," I tease, crouching to her level. "Back again?"

"Daddy said we could walk around for ten minutes while he finishes with the fire truck display." Her voice drops to a whisper, conspiratorial. "What he doesn't know is that I'm buying a secret Christmas spell."

I stifle a laugh. "A secret spell, huh? For you or someone else?"

Her eyes darted to where Theo, her dad, was talking to the festival committee members near the bonfire. Even in a crowd like this, he stands out. His broad shoulders beneath a navy jacket, tousled brown hair catching the glow of holiday lights, and that easy smile that makes my pulse skip a beat.

"For Daddy," Sophia whispers. "He's lonely. He thinks he hides it, but I can feel it."

It's a strange thing, how her words tighten something warm and aching inside me. I packaged a small charm made of rose quartz for love, thyme for courage, and mistletoe for attracting love before handing it over. "This one's special," I say softly. "But remember, magic works best when the heart is open."

Sophia beams. "Then it'll definitely work."

As she scampers off. Hexley flicks his tail and lets out a low, and approving purr. "Don't start," I murmured. "I'm not falling for the firefighter."

But when Theo glances over and catches my eye... his warm amber gaze lingering a second too long... I'm not so sure anymore.

Theo

Sophia's bouncing back toward me with that mischievous glint in her eye that I know all too well. Which means I'm probably about to be roped into something really ridiculous.

"How was the witchy booth?" I ask as she tugs on my jacket.

"Magical," she declares. "Ivy says magic needs an open heart."

I chuckle. "Did she now?"

I've noticed Ivy around before. Really hard not to with that Strawberry-blonde hair that catches fire under the Christmas lights. Her emerald eyes that always seem to see straight through the walls I keep carefully in place. She's sunshine wrapped in mystery, and every time I pass her shop on Main Street, I find an excuse to slow down.

But dating? That's complicated. I've got a six-year-old to raise, a demanding job at the firehouse, and a messy divorce in my rearview mirror. Romance is a luxury I'm not sure I can afford.

Still, when she waves at Sophia then at me something in my chest shifts. When Sophia starts tugging me toward Ivy's booth again, I don't resist.

"Hi there," Ivy greets, her voice a warm breeze against the winter chill. "Sophia's becoming my favorite customer."

"She's very persuasive," I admit, my lips tugging into a smile.

"Wonder where she gets that from." The tease in her tone makes me laugh. A true deep and genuine sound I haven't heard from myself in a while.

Before I could think too hard about it, Cade and Noelle approach. Cade was head of logistics, and from the looks of it looked like he's aged ten years trying to keep the festival running. Noelle, on the other hand, is clearly the reason for at least half of his headaches. Especially judging by the way she's sneaking hot cocoa onto a "no drinks beyond this point" areas.

"You two competing in the wreath toss later this week?" Cade asks.

"Wreath toss?" Ivy tilts her head.

"Annual friendly competition," Noelle explains. "Loser buys the winner a round at Frosty's Tavern."

Sophia's grin is immediate and wicked. "Daddy, we're so doing it."

Ivy's smile matches hers. "Guess we're rivals then."

And just like that, it's not a question of if I'll see her again, but when.

Sparks and Spells

Ivy

It's the third day of the festival and I'm fairly certain I've seen Theo and Sophia more than anyone else. They stop by every morning for cocoa, swung by my booth during lunch, and somehow manage to appear whenever Cade and Noelle start bickering. Which lately, it was often.

Every time Theo's warm amber eyes meet mine, my stomach does a little flip I pretend to try and ignore.

"Stop overthinking it," Stella says beside me as she adjusts the display at her pastry booth. "He's cute, you're cute, and Sophia is basically shipping you two already."

"I don't date firefighters," I lied.

"Why?" She says challenging me.

"Because they're too busy saving the world to date witches."

She rolls her eyes. "Maybe they need someone magical to come home to."

Before I could retort, Theo himself strolls up with Sophia perched on his shoulders. She was giggling as she pointed out holiday decorations like she's never seen a wreath before.

"Morning, Ivy," he greets, voice low and warm.

"Morning, hero," I tease before I can stop myself. His grin is devastating.

We had a small talk. Mostly about the weather, the bonfire lighting, and the snowstorm rolling in. But somewhere between casual banter and shared laughter, I feel the edges of something deeper forming.

When Sophia insisted I join them for the tree-lighting ceremony that night, I didn't even hesitate.

Theo

She said yes. That's all I can think about as we walk toward the town square later. Sophia's mittened hand in one of my hands, and Ivy's is in the other. It feels... right. Easy. Like we're a family, even if we're not.

The square was packed, the massive evergreen tree was strung with gold and red lights. Sophia's eyes shined as the countdown began.

"Three!"
"Two!"
"One!"

The tree bursts into full light and the crowd erupts in cheers. Ivy laughs, and the sound wraps around me, warm and bright.

My throat constricts as we walk toward the cocoa stand. "Thank you," I finally manage.

"For what?" Her voice cuts through the freezing air.

"For saying yes." The words feel inadequate, pathetic even.

Her cheeks flush crimson, and I can't tear my eyes away. "You're welcome, firefighter." The way she says it... low, almost a whisper. It ignites something primal in me.

My heart hammers against my ribs. I want to devour her, protect her, and possess her all at once and forever.

Rules, Rivals, and Almost Kisses

Ivy

Morning snow fell like sifted sugar over Hollysin Town. I tied an olive green scarf around my neck and set a simmer pot on the back plate of the kettle. It had orange peels, clove, cardamom, and a hint of vanilla. The steam curls into the air and the scent turns my little booth into a warm spell.

Hexley supervises from his favorite crate with the arrogant gravitas of a small lion. He tolerates a small knitted Santa hat on his head for exactly three seconds before flicking it off with a disdainful paw. I laugh and place a pinecone crown beside him instead. The crown meets his approval, but barely.

"Inventory check," I murmured while lining up tea tins and spell kits. Different Love blends, Peaceful hearth, and Courage. As well as clarity items/kits. All the things people want most in December.

Footsteps could be heard crunching across the fresh snow. Sophia appears first. She wears her star stickers on her cheeks and the biggest grin that could power an entire light display. Theo follows closely behind with his gloved hands tucked in the pockets of a navy jacket. His amber eyes catching mine like warm sparks.

"Hi Ms. Ivy, reporting for duty," Sophia says, saluting me. "Daddy and I are here to help with important witchy business."

"Excellent," I answered. "I have top secret work for you. We need to pick three charms for a wish jar that will stay at the festival bonfire until the New Year."

Sophia loves every word of that. She hops to the display and studies trays of stones with exaggerated focus. "Rose quartz for love. Snowflake obsidian for balance. Citrine for joy. We definitely need the extra joy."

Theo watches us with a softness that burns through my defenses. He drifts closer, too close, and when he brushes snow from my sleeve... His gloved fingers linger against my arm. The touch detonates through me, igniting every nerve ending until I'm nothing but raw sensation. Woodsmoke and cedar invade my sense. His scent wrapping around me like a vise. I don't just want to lean into him. I want to collapse against him, tear off those damn gloves off with my teeth. To feel his skin against mine. My hands shake with the violent effort of restraint, of not grabbing what belongs to me.

"Wreath toss in five," Cade calls out from the square. His voice carries the weary patience of a man holding the entire town together with a clipboard and sheer stubbornness. "Competitors check in at the north gate."

Noelle skidded onto the path with a contraband cinnamon roll. Cade points at the sign that clearly forbids any food near the games. She gave a sinful smile as she took another bite. He groans, rubbing his temples. They walked off arguing, which for those two is a love language waiting to happen.

Stella hustles by with a tray of cranberry bars. Her hair tucked into a beret, and her cheeks pink with the cold. She spotted me and tilted her head toward the ice carving area. "Kris is already there breaking rules," she huffs. "He keeps carving outside the perimeter because he says the light is better. Who does that."

I followed her gaze towards Kris. He lifts a hand in greeting that is equal parts rude and flirtatious. Stella narrows her eyes like a cat about to pounce. Enemies to lovers, the words whisper through my thoughts, unspoken but certain. I marked them both as acquaintances in my mental ledger of festival regulars.

Sophia yanks my sleeve so hard I nearly topple sideways. "Team Wilder versus Witchlings," she announces with a dramatic hair flip. "Us Witchlings are gonna crush everyone, including my dad, so bad the'll need to invent a new spell for wounded pride."

Theo gives me a crooked smile that should not even be legal. "Careful, I'm basically a professional. They train us for this at the firehouse."

"Is that so?" I tease, tilting my head. "Then I hope you're ready, because witches don't miss. Especially when they want something."

"Then I guess I should hope I'm the target," he says. His gaze dipped to my lips and then back up to my eyes. "Because I don't mind getting hit."

We walk to the game lanes. Laughter floats throughout the crowd. The target poles are set at varying distances with jingling bells tied near the tops. The rules were simple:

Rings on poles.

Bells for bonus points.

The loser buys the winner a drink at Frosty's Tavern.

Noelle announces the last rule twice and may as well have been winking at Cade the whole time.

Sophia stands between us, bouncing. "Ready. Set. Toss."

Theo's first throw arcs high and lands with a clean ring that sets the bell chiming. The sound slides down my spine like a shiver. My first toss lands snugly against the base of the pole. We play to the soundtrack of distant carols and crisp bells ringing. People would cheer. Our shoulders bumped together occasionally. His gloved hand would brush mine in a caressing way when we traded wreaths and neither of us moved away from the other.

By the final round we are tied. Cade clears his throat. Noelle grins around another forbidden treat.

"Bonus challenge," Cade says. "One throw each from the far mark."

"The winner gets bragging rights," Noelle adds. "And a mistletoe coupon redeemable at any time."

A murmur rolls through the crowd. Sophia clasps her hands under her chin. Her eyes bright with hope, big enough to hush the wind.

Theo meets my gaze and a shot of heat pulses low in my belly. We walk to the far mark side by side. He tosses. The wreath sails through falling snow and lands perfectly. As the bell sings, that heat turns into pride for him.

It was my turn. I inhaled and tasted cinnamon, and the metallic promise of coming snow. I pictured the line. I pictured the landing, and then I threw. The wreath flies true and skims the top of the pole. It holds. The bell trembles and then speaks with a delicate silver chime.

Tied again.

Noelle throws her hands up. "Clearly fate wants the coupon to be shared."

Sophia cheers so loud that Hexley actually lifts his head and meows in protest. I laughed until I felt dizzy, and so did Theo.

The crowd thinned out. Cade was scolding Noelle for all her crumbs. She brushes sugar off his jacket with gentle hands and he goes quiet for a moment. It was as if the contact knocked the wind out of all his complaints. Stella announced that she will not speak to Kris again for at least an hour. Kris told her to save him a cranberry bar anyway.

Theo and I drifted toward the edge of the square with Sophia skipping ahead of us. We ended up beneath a cluster of mistletoe woven with little white lights. My skin begins to prickle. The coupon burns a hole in my pocket like a secret.

He looked down at me and his smile fades into something more smoldering and hungry. "So what's it gonna be," he asks, voice a dark rumble. "Do we give in now… or savor the anticipation?"

"Tempting," I breathe, pulse skipping as I meet his gaze. "But I think I like the torture." I turn away with a teasing smile. "Sophia, sweetheart, how about some cocoa?"

Sophia throws her hands up. "At this rate, I'll be old enough to drive before you two figure it out."

I glance at the mistletoe again. We are close enough to taste the same air. He raises one gloved hand to push a stray curl behind my ear. The touch was so gentle. A promise without pressure. I want to kiss him, but I also want to keep wanting him a little longer. The slow burn was its own magic.

"Later," I whisper softly.

The word feels like a match, small and bright. He smiles like a man who knows how to tend to a fire.

Theo

I am not a patient man. Never have been. Firefighting burns that out of you. It trains your body to lunge toward danger while others run away. But wanting Ivy? It's pure torture. A slow searing agony. The need for her blazes through me, white-hot and relentless. It was scorching beneath my skin until I'm nothing but raw nerve endings and desperate hunger.

I turn my attention back to my daughter. Sophia cradles a mug between her small hands, her breath turning the surface of the cocoa into swiling patterns. I crave moments like this. Something so simple, warm, and ordinary. Marshmallow foam clings to Sophia's upper lip as she takes a careful sip. She tells Ivy that the snow is coming early this year because the sky wants to be festive. Ivy doesn't laugh or brush her off. She nodded, meeting Sophia's gaze in earnest agreement. Ivy always treated my girl like her feelings mattered, like every word she says has weight. It makes my chest ache, in the best and worst way.

We walked Ivy back to her booth. Hexley slinked across the table like a familiar who has seen every secret anyone ever tried to keep. Ivy fastens the stall flap and locks the cash box. She glanced up at the sky, pausing for a moment, then looked at me.

"The wind's brewing trouble tonight," she murmurs, gaze drifting toward the darkening sky.

"Yeah," I say. "Feels like a big one."

"Will you be working when it hits?" she said, biting her lip in worry.

"On call," I replied. "If the roads turn treacherous… or someone's candle magic gets out of hand."

Her eyes glinting like she's hiding a secret. "My candles know how to mind their magic."

"I know," I say, a ghost of a smile tugging at my lips. "I can smell the calm in them."

We fall quiet and there is a pull between us as steady as a tide. I noticed new things when I let myself look fully at her. Between the pierced hoop in her ear with a tiny crescent, to the ink on her forearm that curls under her sleeves. The way her scarf sets off the green in her eyes. I wanted to memorize all of it… all of her.

"Dinner," Sophia announces. "Daddy, you promised me pizza."

I blinked and refocused. "I did promise you."

Ivy smiles that soft, private smile again. "Go. I will see you at the bonfire later. If the weather holds, that is."

If the weather was kind. But the sky has other plans. As dusk deepens, fat flakes tumble from the sky, and Jingle Jack's voice bursts through the town radio like a jolly alarm. "Ho-ho-hold onto your hats, Hollysin! This storm's clocking in ahead of schedule and bringing enough snow to make Frosty jealous. Stay safe, keep the cocoa hot, and maybe light a candle or two."

With the storm's arrival confirmed, Cade reluctantly delays the bonfire, and then bumps the carol singing to tomorrow. Noelle steals the microphone from him to remind everyone to drive slow and to wear hats. Stella hides under the pastry tent and throws shade at Kris in the group chat because his ice carving is now art under a white blanket and he is smug about it.

The drive home was quiet, the world outside dimming under a

blanket of white. By the time we pulled into the driveway, the streetlights glowed in soft halos. Snow clung to the brim of Sophia's hat as she hops out. Her laughter echoed in the stillness. Inside, the house had its own pocket of warmth against the growing storm. Sophia pressed her nose to the window, her breath fogging up the glass as she hums a tune only she knows. She was tracing spirals and stars into the frost with her small fingertips. I slip into my routine, checking the truck's engine, stacking the salt near the porch, and leaning the shovel where I can grab it quickly. The overnight bag waited faithfully by the door. Always packed for whatever the job might throw at me that day. Then I paused, just breathing it all in. The faint sound of the crackle of the wood fire, the lingering scent of pizza, and the sweet peppermint smell of the cookies we had baked last weekend. It was simple, and imperfect. It's home... well almost home.

At that moment my phone buzzes.

Cade.

The electrical heater line failed in one of the vendor rows. No open flame, no smoke, not an emergency yet. But if the line is out and the wind is that fierce, they need to be quickly checked.

"I have to swing by the square," I tell Sophia. "You can come or you can stay with Mrs. Payne next door."

She turns from the window. "Can I come if we can go by Ivy's shop after. I want to give Hexley his present."

"What present?"

She digs around in her pocket and then produces a felt mouse with a single glitter star glued onto its back. "A Charm mouse."

I want to tell her we cannot detour. The roads will be bad and slick. The wind will be even worse by each passing minute. I wanted to say it but I did not. Only because I can see how much she wants to and because I also want to make that detour too.

"Okay, but only for a minute."

We bundled up and stepped into the kind of night that made you feel small in the best way. Snowflakes as big as peppermint wafers feathered down. The wind was a steady whisper, and the town lights turned the falling white into a thousand soft diamonds.

The square looked like a ghost town but in a beautiful way. Cade met me with a flashlight and was wearing a stubborn expression. He and I get the heater line secured long enough for the maintenance crew to arrive. Noelle appears with extra hats and hand warmers. She had zero fear of rules about restricted areas. She tucked a hat onto Cade's head with a bossy sort of tenderness. He allowed it without protest. For them this counts as a kiss.

We finished up and I texted Ivy to see if she was still at the shop. She texted back saying that she was. She warned me to drive slow, which I already was.

Her storefront glowed like a warm hearth in the storm. Golden light poured behind frosted windows. A hand painted sign with evergreen garlands. My pulse raced as I guided Sophia inside.

Ivy came out from the back of the store, and the heat of her presence kisses my chilled skin. The place smells like everything good. Vanilla, herbs, pine, and tea. Hexley sat on the counter like the prince of winter.

Sophia rushes to present the charm mouse. Hexley batted it once and then claimed it as a personal friend. Ivy laughs and the sound melts the cold straight out of my bones.

"The storm's turning mean," I say, watching the wind claw at the streetlights. "We should leave before it decides to trap us."

She nodded, eyes narrowing as if she could read the storm's

intent in the way the snow curls against the windowpane. The door groans under a sudden blast of wind. The light sputters and steadies... Once, Twice, almost like a candle fighting to stay lit.

In that moment, as if the night has casted a spell of its own, the shop slips into shadows.

For a breath the shop becomes a paper theater of shadows and moonlight. Then Ivy moves with grace and calm. She lights beeswax tapers with a long match, and the place blooms into honeyed golden light. The ceiling gleams with strings of stars, and the tea jars turn to small stained glass jewels.

"You okay?" I asked.

"I am always prepared for the winter," she says with a smile. "Are you two okay?"

Sophia nodded but steps closer to me. The wind whistles against the door. The heater clicks but does not catch.

"Backup heat," Ivy says briskly. She moves behind the counter pulling out a small ceramic heater and a copper kettle from a lower shelf. She sets both near the candle cluster on a safe tile slab. She is so efficient and calm. I take a moment to appreciate her beauty in the candlelight. It shouldn't undo me the way it does, but it does. She was so damn beautiful that it hurt.

"We should stay put until the plows clear the roads," I said while glancing back toward the storm raging outside. "No point in risking it with the power out and the wind howling."

"I was hoping you'd say that," she replies softly. "You'll both be safe here. I promise."

Sophia picks a bean bag chair from the reading nook and curls up with a throw blanket. Ivy made her a mild lavender tea sweetened with honey and a tiny star shaped sugar. They whispered about stories and cats until Sophia's eyes drooped and her breathing turned slow and even.

It was late now, probably nearing midnight. The storm pressed against the windows like a steady hand. The candlelight flickers when the wind gusts make its way from the cracks under the shop doors. We sat at the small table near the herbs. Ivy pours me a stronger tea. The steam warmed my face. Her knee brushes mine under the table and stays.

Her gaze drifts down my arm, soft and curious. It lingered on the ink just visible beneath the edge of my sleeve.

"Your tattoo," she murmurs, almost like it's a secret between us. "Can I see it?"

I push the fabric back, exposing the small design etched into my skin. A single matchstick, the flame looked like it flickered at its tip. It's simple, clean, and a quiet promise inked into flesh. It was a reminder to light what matters most and keep it burning.

She studies it for a long moment. Her eyes tracing the shape with something that feels a lot like understanding before lifting to meet mine. "That suits you," she says, and there's something deeper in her tone. Almost like she's not just talking about the tattoo.

My gaze falls to the ink curling over her own skin, peeking from beneath the edge of her sleeve. "And yours?"

She removed the sweater revealing a camisole underneath in that olive green that matched her scarf. She extended her arm, letting me see it fully. Vines coil delicately across her skin, stars scattered between them. A crescent moon nestled near her wrist, and there, hidden in the leaves, a fox mid-prowl. The art felt alive, breathing its own quiet story. I lift a hand, tracing the air just above it. Just close enough to feel the warmth of her skin without touching.

"That suits you too," I murmured, and I mean all of it.

Silence folded around us, soft as snowfall. Not heavy. Just... full.

"I like you, Theo," she says finally, voice barely louder than the storm's distant hum. "I didn't expect to. I wasn't planning to. But I do."

My chest tightens, the words catching somewhere between my heart and my throat. "I like you too," I admit. The truth was heavier than I meant it to be. "More than what is probably wise."

We sit with the truth of that for a long moment. Then Sophia exhales a dreamy sigh and murmurs from the nook. "Use the coupon," she mumbles from sleep. "You can always get more mistletoe."

We both laugh, quiet and helpless. Ivy stands and moves to the doorway of the reading nook to tuck the blanket around Sophia. When she turns back to me, her eyes are darker. The air between us feels like the inch of space just above a flame.

"Come here," I say. My voice was low and rough. A command dressed up like a request.

Her breath catches, and for a heartbeat she doesn't move. Then she does. One slow, deliberate step, then another, until the space between us is gone and the air is heavy with everything we haven't said.

I rise to meet her, close enough now to feel the warmth of her body radiating. My hand lifted, fingers brushing her jaw, and tracing the line of her neck before settling beneath her chin. I tilted her face up, holding her there. Not trapping, just guiding, a silent question hanging between us.

Her eyes flick to my mouth and back again. That's all the answer I needed.

When I finally closed the distance between us, the kiss wasn't hesitant... It was deliberate. Slow, yes, but laced with intent. With a hunger I've been fighting since the moment I met her. Our lips meet, soft at first, a curious press, a breath shared, and then deeper. Like something breaking open. She tasted faintly of honey and peppermint, sweet and wild all at once. The soft sound she made against my mouth nearly undoes me.

Her fingers slide into my hair, tentative at first, then bolder. I respond in kind, palms tightening at her waist as I pull her closer. Until there's no space left to hide. Her heartbeat thumps fast against my chest. Mine pounds just as hard to match.

I angle the kiss deeper, taking my time with it. Learning the shape of her mouth like I plan to memorize every inch. It was careful and consuming all at once. Not just a kiss, but a claim, a beginning to us.

When we finally break apart, the world feels changed. It was quieter somehow, except for the storm howling against the windows and the thunder of my pulse in my ears. She stayed close, her breath mingling with mine, and eyes wide and dazed.

"Later," she whispers, the word trembling between us. "Slow. I want to go slow."

I brush my thumb over her bottom lip that was swollen and kiss-stung. "Then slow's exactly what I'll give you," I murmured. My voice was still low and rough. "But this... this is just the start."

We stay like that. Breath to breath, skin humming, while the storm rages outside. I knew in that moment, without a doubt that nothing about us will ever be the same again.

The Long Night and the Match

Ivy

I wake near dawn with my head on Theo's shoulder, and a blanket pulled over both of us in the reading nook. The candles have burned low to golden cups. The storm had quieted to a hush. Sophia was snoring like a small ferocious kitten.

I do not remember falling asleep. I remembered the toe curling kiss. I remembered the feel of his hand steady at my waist and the way he breathed my name like a spell. I remembered how careful he was with me, and I remembered the greedy part of me that wanted to be less careful and more now.

I stood and stretched. Theo blinks awake and stares at me like he is not sure if he is still dreaming. He smiles and it is a slow sunrise in human form.

"Morning," he says, voice rough with sleep.

"Morning yourself."

The power clicks back to life with a hum. The heater rumbles. The lights blink on and my shop returns to its ordinary magic. I set the water to boil for tea. Theo checks his phone for any storm updates. Sophia sits up and yawns. Her hair has grown a halo of static from the blanket. She beams when she sees us both within reach.

"Best sleepover ever," she declares.

We drink tea and eat some shortbread. The world outside is sugared and blue. I should open the booth in two hours, but a part of me wants to lock the door and spend the rest of the entire day against Theo's chest.

Sophia starts a puzzle with Hexley's unhelpful assistance. Theo strides towards the window, and checks the sidewalks. Then returns to me with that look again. The kind with blazing heat and deep desire.

"Would you like to join us for lunch after we check in on the square," he asks. "We can help Cade if he needs it and then grab something at Mabel's Maple Cafe."

"I would like that," I say, and it is the simple truth.

We bundled up and stepped into a morning that smells like clean slate. Fluffy snow. New light. The square is already bustling. Cade looks like a man who won a battle in the night. Noelle moves beside him in a puffy blue coat and a look of sunshine victory. Their bickering has changed timbre. There is a fondness under every complaint. I pretend not to notice when their hands brush and stay.

Stella hands out free samples to anyone who shoveled the paths. Kris carries salt and pretends he did not also bring Stella her coffee exactly right. They shoot annoyed looks at each other that are only annoyed if you ignore their smiles. Acquaintances, I note again. Very spirited acquaintances.

Sophia delivers a status update to anyone who will listen. "We survived the storm at Ivy's shop. The candles were cooperative. Hexley is now best friends with a charm mouse." She leans closer. "Daddy and Ivy are using the mistletoe coupon responsibly."

Heat flooded my face. Theo laughed and rested a hand at the small of my back. The touch felt protective and present. I liked it more than I should have.

Lunch at Mabel's turns into a booth for three near the window while the sun melts icicles into glittering drops. We share pancakes and bacon. Sophia dunks everything in maple syrup with an artist's intensity. When a couple at a nearby table recognizes Theo from the firehouse and thanks him for clearing a branch from their roof during the night, he blushes and tries to wave it off. I do not wave it off. I keep my hand on his thigh under the table and give him quiet credit in the form of a light squeeze.

We walked back through town after, our bellies full and hearts lighter. Cade tells me the bonfire and carol singing is rescheduled for tonight if the wind stays calm. He asked if I would lead the wish jar ceremony after the first song. I agreed. He adds a quiet thank you because I delivered tea to the maintenance crew during the worst of the storm. I tell him to thank Noelle because she delivered the extra hats. He mutters that she needs to stop breaking rules. The way he looks at her says he hopes she never does.

The afternoon blurs into festival work. I sell tea and charms. I taught a tourist how to string protection garland for her new apartment. I slipped extra cinnamon sticks into the bag for an elderly man who wanted his kitchen to smell like the Christmases his late wife loved. Theo and Sophia visited often and each time they do, the air seems brighter.

Dusk slides in like velvet. People gathered with mugs and scarves. The bonfire roars alive with a whoosh that makes everyone cheer. The flames are tall and eager. I felt them on my face and I closed my eyes. The fire, heat, and a wish. I caught a glimpse of Theo out of my peripheral vision. His eyes reflect the fiery blaze, and every wish I have condenses into one.

Cade calls for quiet. Noelle stands beside him and bumps his shoulder like a secret. I step forward with my wish jar. Three stones glimmer inside. Joy. Protection. Love.

"Welcome back to the light," I say to the crowd. "If you have a wish for the season, whisper it. If you have a burden, whisper that too, and let it fall away. Everything you offer will burn in kindness."

The words are simple and true. People murmur into their scarves. A few wipe tears. Children clasp mittened hands and close their eyes. I look at Theo and find him already looking at me. My breath goes shallow. He mouths one word.

You.

I swallowed hard and smiled. The slow burn has done its job. I am already set aflame.

The music starts. People started singing. I am not sure who touches whom first. I know the first brush of his fingers against mine felt inevitable. He draws me slightly aside behind a curtain of tall snow pines decorated with white lights. Snow softens the world around us and our breath makes small puffs of clouds in the dark.

"Come home with me after," he says. So quiet so only I could hear. "Sophia wants to build a blanket fort and she wants you there. I want you there. I also want you later when the fort turns into sleep."

"Yes," I whisper. No hesitation in my voice. "Yes."

Sophia catches us on the way to the truck with maple candy in both hands. She gives one to me and one to Theo, informing us that she already packed a to-go bag for Hexley that contains the charm mouse and a collapsible bowl. Ivy the witch and Theo the firefighter cannot argue with logistics that perfect.

We build the fort together in the living room, with all the quilts, and the soft glow of lamps. Sophia was an architect, and Theo followed her directions with careful attention. It breaks me a little in the best way.

We read a story. We drink warm milk. Sophia crawls into the fort and falls asleep with the charm mouse tucked under her chin. Hexley chooses the ottoman like a furry chaperone. Theo checks that the door is locked and that the stove is off. Double checking that the world we have made is safe.

Then we stand in the half light of the hallway, facing each other.

"Come here," he says again, voice rough with need.

I go, already wet with anticipation.

He devours me, tongue demanding entrance. There is no hesitation as he backs me against the wall, one thigh pressing between my legs. He grips my hair and pulls, exposing my neck to his teeth. My core throbs when he bites down, marking me. I claw beneath his shirt, desperate for skin. I found the hard planes of his chest, the trail of hair leading down. Strong. Thick. Mine for the taking. He growls when I grasp his hardness through the denim. The sound makes me clench with emptiness.

We stumbled to his bedroom, tearing at each other's clothes. Buttons scatter. Fabric tearing. He throws me onto the mattress. His eyes dark with hunger as he strips naked. His cock stands proud, flushed and ready. I spread my legs in invitation. He drops to his knees instead, dragging me to the edge. His tongue finds my center with devastating precision, circling, and flicking. He devoured me until I was writhing and begging for release. He pushed two thick fingers inside, curling them until they found that sweet spot that made me scream his name.

I flipped us, straddling him, and sinking down inch by delicious inch until he filled me completely. The stretch burned so good I cried out again. He grips my ass hard enough to bruise, guiding me into a punishing rhythm. I ride him mercilessly, watching his face contort with pleasure. Sweat slicks our bodies as we chase our release together. His thumb finds my clit again, and rubs tight circles that make my vision blur.

When I cum, it's violent. My body convulses, walls clamping down on him like a vise. He flips me onto my back, pounding relentlessly through my aftershocks until he stiffens. He groaned as he emptied himself deep inside me. My name a filthy prayer on his lips.

We stay tangled through the aftershocks of pleasure and the glow of happiness. I pressed my lips to his shoulder and he stroked my hair slowly.

We do not go to sleep right away. We talked in the soft dark instead. He tells me that he was scared to want this. I told him I was too. He tells me about the hurt he carries. About leaving things unsaid because he does not want to scare anyone away with the size of his love. I tell him I do not scare easily. He laughs and says he knows that already.

Sometime after midnight, I drifted off. The last thing I feel is his breath warm against my neck and the weight of his arm around my waist holding me against him like I am not something he expects to lose.

Mistletoe and Matches

Theo

The next morning smells like coffee and cinnamon toast. The sun glinting off of the last snow on the porch rail. Sophia hums in the kitchen while she builds a tower of apple slices and peanut butter. Hexley patrols the counter like a furry health inspector. Ivy stands at my stove in my shirt. I will never recover from this vision, my heart literally stops as I start getting hard again.

She turns with a plate for me and a plate for herself. Her eyes were bright and hair in that post sex look. "Eat," she orders. "You have a long day of fatherhood and festival heroics ahead."

"Yes, ma'am," I say. I am smiling like a fool and I do not care.

Sophia looks up from her architectural breakfast. She studies both of us with a solemn air that is all too knowing. Then she grins and points to her front teeth, or rather the space where they are not. "You used the coupon responsibly," she says.

I choked on my coffee and Ivy chokes on her toast. We recovered as best we could while Sophia pats Hexley and sings to him about charm mice and love spells. The laughter lingers like a blessing over everything.

We spent the morning doing ordinary things that felt like magic because we were doing them together. We shoveled out sidewalks and driveways, checked in on neighbors, and carried wood to Mrs Payne's porch. She gave us a tin of fudge so sweet it makes my teeth tingle. We stopped by the firehouse to switch duty gear out for clean gear. The guys gave me a look that shifts from teasing to approving when they meet Ivy and see how Sophia lights up around her.

By late afternoon the festival is in full swing again. Cade looks less stressed. Noelle looks guilty for five seconds, before stealing a cinnamon twist and getting powdered sugar all over his scarf. He pretends to be annoyed, but kisses her in front of the cider stand. The crowd cheers. He blushes and then shrugs like a man who has finally accepted that rules do not matter when your heart is on the line.

Stella and Kris run the friendly competition board together. They argued about scoring and end up laughing so hard that Stella drops her pencil and Kris pockets it like a trophy. They were acquaintances the way a match and a striker are acquaintances.

Sophia takes charge of our schedule with the seriousness of a committee chair. We decorate a gingerbread house that wins Most Enthusiastic Use of Sprinkles. We watch the skating show and clap for a kid who nails a tiny jump. We tossed snowballs at the inflatable reindeer target and won two candy canes, as well as a plush snowflake that Sophia promptly named it Captain Flurry.

Ivy's booth is the heart of my day. She moved through her space with a grace that is part dance, and part ritual. People lean toward her and soften in her presence. She listens with her whole being. She sells tea and charms, yes, but it was more than that. She sold the belief that the world can still be kind. Watching her work makes me want to be better at mine. It makes me want to be better in general.

The sun slips low and paints the square in a rose gold color. Cade lifted the mic to announce the final friendly event. The Lantern Walk. Families and couples collect paper lanterns sparked by long matches. We will circle the square, end at the bonfire, and release wishes into the night.

Noelle hands Sophia a lantern with stars cut into the sides. "For the bravest kid I know," she says. She hands me a lantern with a wobbly snowman drawn on one panel, and hands Ivy a lantern trimmed with green ribbon. The ribbon matches Ivy's eyes.

We light the lanterns together. Ivy touches her flame to mine and something quiet lifts in my chest. We begin the walk. The sky darkens to a deep indigo with our lanterns glowing like warm moons. Christmas carols rise and fall all around us. The threads of sound weaving through the cold.

Sophia walks between us, holding our hands. She swings our arms and hums. She tips her face up. "I have a wish," she says. "But I think it already came true."

"What is it," Ivy asks.

Sophia squeezes our hands. "I wanted our house to feel full again."

My throat goes tight, and I squeeze back. Ivy looks at me with tears shining in her eyes and nods. She understands. She always does.

We reach the bonfire. Cade gives a signal and the crowd falls quiet. One by one, lanterns began to lift and drift. They were tethered to lines that hold them in a circle of light. Wishes were whispered into the sky. I look at Ivy and know this is the moment I do not let pass.

"I want this," I say, quiet but sure, so only Ivy and Sophia can hear. "I want you in our life. Not just for the holidays. For real."

Ivy's breath catches, and her smile trembles in the way that wrecks me a little. "Good," she says softly. "Because I want the whole thing too. Morning pancakes. Blanket forts. Hexley knocking ornaments off the tree. Late-night kisses. School drop-offs. All of it."

Before either of us can blink, Sophia lets out a delighted squeal and flings herself between us like a tiny missile of joy. "Finally!" she declares. "Took you both long enough!"

We burst out laughing, the three of us tangled in coats and arms and snowflakes. Above us, the lanterns drifted like little suns, and for the first time in a long time, my heart feels exactly where it belongs. Loud, bright, and completely out of rhythm in the best way.

The crowd begins to move again. The mistletoe arch from the wreath toss has been set back up beside the cider stand. Noelle sees us and wiggles her brows in the least subtle way possible. Cade pretends not to see her and then clears his throat. "New tradition," he calls out. "Kiss under the arch to seal your wishes."

I glance at Ivy with a question. She answers with a smile that is both shy and bold. We step under the mistletoe and lights while Sophia stands on tiptoe in front of us, hands clasped, eyes looking earnest.

"Do the coupon," she whispers. "But like in a ceremony."

I seize Ivy's face between my hands. The world vanishes. There's only her mouth, her breath hot against mine. I crush my lips to hers, claiming her. Not for show, but as a vow. The fire erupts between us as she presses against me until there's no space left, our bodies remembering each other. The crowd's roar crashes over us like a tidal wave, but we're drowning willingly in each other.

"Home," I say.

"Home," she echoes.

We end the night in my living room with the fort rebuilt and the fire murmuring. Sophia crafts place cards for the three of us. Hexley occupies the center cushion like a sovereign. We sipped on peppermint cocoa. Ivy leans into me and I tuck her closer.

"Tell me a story," Sophia says, drowsy but determined.

I look at Ivy. She smiles, amused. I clear my throat and let the words come.

"Once there was a girl," I say, "with green eyes like the first leaves of spring. She made tea that could comfort a storm, and charms that could brave a long night. She kept a cat who was a prince in disguise, and she taught a tired firefighter that some fires are meant to be tended. Not put out."

Sophia sighs, satisfied. "Good story."

Ivy kisses the side of my neck, soft and sure. "Best story."

We tuck Sophia into bed for the night with Hexley curling up by her feet.

Later when the house was quiet and the tree lights pulsed like a heartbeat, I seized Ivy's hand and pulled her down the hall. We tear at each other's clothes, ravenous now where we were once uncertain. We know the map of each other's bodies by heart. We devour each moment because we've waited lifetimes for this. The second time ignites like wildfire. My teeth graze her collarbone and she claws at my back. Her trust was like a drug I couldn't get enough of. She claimed me with merciless precision and I surrendered completely. My tenderness transformed to desperation. When she shatters she screams my name like salvation. When I follow, hers tears from my throat like a prayer I've been holding in for years.

After, we lie quietly, breathing the same air, our fingers laced. I trace the crescent on her arm and picture a future I am suddenly brave enough to plan. Breakfasts. School days. Late shifts and tea waiting when I get home. Festival seasons. Maybe a summer at the lake. Definitely a lifetime of lighting matches that matter.

"Let us write it down," Ivy whispers in the dark. "A list. Not rules, but our hopes."

"Okay," I say. "Hope one. Keep choosing this, even on tired days."

"Hope two," she answers. "Make room for wonder."

"Hope three," I say. "Always keep a mistletoe coupon in the junk drawer."

She laughs into my chest. "Deal."

I kiss the top of her head. The window burns with a harsh square of winter moon, casting shadows across her skin. I dragged my finger hard along her collarbone, and she jolts back awake. Her eyes flashing with ravenous need. We crash together again, cinnamon and clove searing our skin from earlier. The taste of her neck was fierce and intoxicating against my desperate tongue. Later, the house groans like a wounded animal that has finally found release. Hexley slams onto the foot of the bed and rumbles with a thunderous purr that vibrates through our exhausted bodies.

I hold my witch close, her skin cool against my fingertips. Her breath went back to a gentle rhythm against my collarbone. She holds me back, arms wrapped around my waist, and her face nestled in the hollow spot of my neck. We fall asleep sure of the same thing. Our bodies curved together like two halves of a locket.

This is home.

Epilogue: One Week Later

Ivy

The Mistletoe Mischief Festival winds down under a sky the color of sugar cookies. Cade and Noelle slow dance near the empty cocoa stand and pretend no one can see. Stella and Kris announce a pop up bake and carve night that is absolutely not a date. People stopped by my booth to say thank you and buy tea for the new year. Hexley signs exactly three pawtographs. Do not ask.

Theo arrives with Sophia, both wearing paper crowns from the craft table. Sophia presents me with an official festival committee pin. Chosen by small hands, she says gravely. I pin it to my scarf and tear up instantly like the softhearted witch I am.

Theo kisses me under the last sprig of mistletoe hanging from the wrought-iron lamppost in the cobblestone square. It was not an almost kiss, like the brush of shoulders in the bookshop doorway. It was not a maybe, like our fingers grazing over spiced cider mugs. It was the beginning and the middle, and the later we promised each other beneath a sky dusted with stars like sugar.

He leans in close, his breath warm against my winter-chilled skin. Murmuring against my mouth, "I love you," his voice was deep and rough that catches on something deep inside me.

The world tilts sweetly, Christmas lights blurring into golden halos. "I love you too."

Sophia claps her mittened hands together, her cheeks flushed pink with cold and delight. Hexley meows like a benediction, his brown tail curling around my ankle. Bells ring from the stone church on the hill, their bronze voices echoing across the frost-tipped rooftops. The wind carries the scent of cinnamon and snow, of pine needles and woodsmoke curling from chimneys.

Hollysin Town hums with the kind of magic that does not ask to be believed. It lives in the spaces between heartbeats and holiday wishes. It simply was.

And so are we.

Bonus Chapter!

Hexley's Secret Journal of Hollysin Nonsense.

Day 1 of the Festival: The human, Ivy, is fussing again. Candles, herbs, and sparkly trinkets... So many things cluttering my napping surfaces. She says she's *"arranging the booth."* I say she's *"ruining perfectly good boxes."*

I try to help, obviously. I lie on the prettiest scarf, the one that smells like patchouli and victory. She moves me. Rude. I meow in protest. Once, twice, then the long, drawn-out **"Mrrrreeeooow"** that always gets results. She calls me dramatic. I call it passion.

Then the big Firefighter walks in. Big human. Smells like smoke, cinnamon gum, and complicated emotions. Ivy's heartbeat does this weird flutter. I stare at him long enough for dominance. He grins at me and says, *"Hey, big guy."*

Excuse me? *Big Guy*? I am majestic. A panther condensed for indoor use.

Still, he scratches behind my ear. Hmf. Acceptable.

Day 2: Tiny human returns. Sophia. The mini-witch. High-pitched voice, sticky fingers, and endless questions. She tries to put a snowflake sticker on my forehead. I tolerate it because she smells like marshmallows and sincerity.

The big human is back too. He and Ivy keep exchanging long looks as if telepathy is new. Their faces do that soft, confused thing that humans call *flirting*. I lick my paw and watch. Someone has to supervise.

Night of the Storm: Wind howls. Lights flicker. I predicted this several hours earlier by hiding under the counter. Ivy ignores my profressional weather alert. Typical.

When the power goes out, they light candles. My candles. MY territory. I sit beside the flames to absorb ambiance. The big human looks at Ivy like she's the only light left in the room. Gross. Romantic.

They talk. They kiss. Finally. I yawn loudly to remind them of priorities: **Feeding me.** They do not notice. Humans are hopeless when pheromones are involved.

The Morning After: Sunlight. Warm Blanket. Two humans asleep on the couch like mismatched kittens. The small one snores. The big one drools. Ivy, smiles in her sleep, with her hand resting near mine. I should move. I don't.

I purr. Just a little. Don't tell anyone. It's bad for my reputation. I inch closer to her fingers. Just to monitor her pulse, of course.

End of Festival Notes: The house now smells like coffee, woodsmoke, and happiness. I approve. The small human built me a crown out of tinsel. The big human calls me *"buddy"*. Ivy keeps whispering thank-yous to the air as if she didn't notice I'm the one who orchestrated all this by sitting in the right box at the right time.

Humans. So needy. So Loud. So warm.

Mrrp. I suppose I'll keep them.

And that is how I, Hexley Marlowe, single-pawed familiar of Hollysin Town, successfully herded two stubborn humans into love. You are welcome. Mrrp.

Now if you'll excuse me, I have ornaments to knock off the tree. Farewell, human reader.

Afterword

And just like that, another winter night in Hollysin Town comes to a close.

When I wrote Mistletoe & Matches, I wanted to create a world that felt like stepping into a snow globe. One that is filled with glittering lights, found family, and a touch of heat strong enough to melt the frost. Ivy and Theo's story reminds me that even in the simplest moments; a kiss under the mistletoe, a snowstorm that changes everything, a child's laughter echoing through candlelight... can be their own kind of magic.

Thank you so much for spending time in Hollysin. For believing in the warmth of small towns, and for letting a witch and a firefighter steal a couple hours of your heart.

The fire's still burning here... and something tells me the next spark is waiting. Check out Stella & Kris's story next in Merry Mischief by Melody A. Rose. The last installment to this trilogy will be Cade & Noelle in Decked & Frosted by Jade D. Hart.

Acknowledgement

This book wouldn't exist without caffeine, chaos, and a few patient humans who let me text them at all hours asking what their thoughts were about the "spicy scenes."

Thank you to my little family for tolerating my "Mommy is working right now, just one more minute," moments. To my friends who never let me quit.

To my readers and reading community: You're the real magic. You showed up, you swooned, you screamed in my DM's, and you make my sleepless nights worth it.

And to anyone who's ever believed that witches deserve love, firefighters deserve softness, and small-towns can still hold magic... this one is for you.

About The Author

Sereyna Vale

Sereyna Vale is an aspiring author with a love for all things twisty, thrilling, and a little bit swoony. Happily married and a full-time stay-at-home mom (to both her kids and her beloved furbabies), she spends her days juggling family life with the wild worlds she creates on the page.

Chances are you'll spot her with a Dr. Pepper or an Alani in hand, snacking on Flamin' Hot Cheetos paired with whipped cream cheese... her not-so-secret writing fuel. A proud Libra and lifelong bookworm. She's a devoted fan of Christine Feehan, Catherine Cowles, and Kelsie Rae.

In the future, readers can expect her books to span genres including Paranormal, Thriller, Romance, and Young Adult. All with unforgettable characters and page-turning plots.

When she's not writing, she's devouring her next read, dreaming up new stories, or hanging out with her family in between chapters.

Books By This Author

Echoes In Sleep

When Sonya mutes her phone to escape the noise, she expects peace, not terror. But when she turns it back on, every missed notification is a video of her sleeping, videos no one should have been able to record. As the messages grow darker and reality begins to fracture, Sonya must confront a chilling truth: the real threat might not be watching from the outside, it could already be in her hands.

A gripping psychological horror novella that blurs the line between technology and madness.

Crimson Veil

Genevieve's graduation party was supposed to be unforgettable, but not like this. One moment she's surrounded by friends, music, and booze. The next, there's blood on the carpet, a blackout, and she's waking up in a hospital with no one believing her story. The house is condemned, her friends are gone, and a hooded figure with a knife, and something far from human keeps showing up. Now she's caught between the world she knows and a place that shouldn't exist, and she has no idea if she's losing her grip… or if something far worse has found her.

Scars We Claim

She inks beauty into the skin of others while hiding the scars etched into her own.

He wears his demons like armor, riding through the night with nothing but a motorcycle and a past he can't outrun.

When their worlds collide, sparks burn hotter than either expected. But passion can't erase pain—and love can't heal what's still bleeding.

Together, they'll have to decide if the scars they carry are what will destroy them… or what will finally make them whole.

Perfect for readers who crave tattooed heroines, broody MC heroes, found family, and love born in the shadows.

Trigger Warnings: Violence, Trauma, Emotional Abuse, Grief, PTSD, and Mature Themes.

Made in the USA
Las Vegas, NV
25 January 2026